WHISPERVEIL

The Light Beyond
A Tale of Courage and Friendship

Jah Kingdom

WhisperVeil: The Light Beyond

Published by Jah Kingdom via Kindle Direct Publishing (KDP).

For permissions or inquiries, please contact: jahmaxkingdom@gmail.com

Paperback ISBN:978-1-968404-20-8

First Edition

To the dreamers, the seekers, and the believers.

May you always find light in the darkness and courage in the face of fear.

"The light shines in the darkness, and the darkness has not overcome it."

(John 1:5, NIV)

Acknowledgments

I want to take a moment to give thanks and express my deepest gratitude:

To my Heavenly Father, thank You for Your unwavering grace, guidance, and strength. Without Your light, none of this would be possible.

To my family and friends, thank you for your encouragement, prayers, and endless support. You inspire me to keep moving forward, even when the path feels uncertain.

To the skeptics in my circle, I love you all. Your skepticism has played a unique role in my journey, pushing me to rise above doubt and empowering me to move forward with faith. Christ Himself faced trials and doubt, and I am reminded daily to wear the armor of Christ and stand firm. As Proverbs says, "Commit to the Lord whatever you do, and He will establish your plans" (Proverbs 16:3, NIV).

To KDP (Kindle Direct Publishing), thank you for giving independent authors like me the tools and platform to share our stories with the world. Your dedication to empowering storytellers has made dreams like mine a reality.

To my readers, this story exists because of you. Thank you for diving into these pages, for believing in my words, and for sharing this journey with me. Your love for stories keeps the light alive, and I'm forever grateful.

About the Author

Jah Kingdom is a storyteller driven by creativity, faith, and a passion for crafting worlds where courage and hope shine through darkness. Jah Kingdom writes under a pseudonym and brings mystery, adventure, and heartfelt connections to life, sharing tales that resonate deeply with readers.

As a firm believer in the Lord Jesus Christ, Jah Kingdom finds inspiration in faith and uses storytelling to explore themes of resilience, friendship, and triumph over fear. This debut novel, Whisperveil: The Light Beyond, is the first step in connecting with readers and sharing stories that uplift and inspire them.

Jah Kingdom holds to the promise of ***Proverbs 3:5–6:*** "Trust in the Lord with all your heart and lean not on your *own* understanding; in all your ways submit to Him, and He will make your paths straight."

When not writing, Jah Kingdom enjoys reflecting on life, exploring new ideas, and finding fresh ways to create meaningful experiences for readers.

Preface

Fear has a way of weaving itself into our lives, whispering doubts into our hearts and convincing us to stay in the shadows. Writing *Whisperveil: The Light Beyond* was my way of confronting those whispers—not just for myself, but for anyone who has ever felt trapped by fear.

This story is about friendship, resilience, and the light that can guide us through the darkness. It's about the courage to face what scares us most, not by fighting alone but by leaning on those who walk alongside us. As a firm believer in Christ, I am inspired by the idea that light shines brightest when it comes from love, unity, and hope.

To every reader who chooses to embark on this journey, thank you. My hope is that Whisperveil: The Light Beyond will inspire you to see the light in your own life and remind you that fear, no matter how strong, does not define who you are.

—Jah Kingdom

Table of Contents

Chapter 1: Whispers in the Manor

Theo, the cautious leader; Zane, the joker of the group; and Aria, the serious and focused one, stood at the edge of the overgrown path, their gazes fixed on the manor's towering, foreboding presence. The fading sunlight cast long shadows across Elmwood Manor's decaying facade. Vines crawled up the cracked stone walls, their tendrils gripping the building like it was their final anchor to life.

"This place looks like it's straight out of a horror movie," Zane muttered, gripping his flashlight. "The kind where everyone dies in the first ten minutes."

Theo glanced at him, the faint flicker of a smirk breaking through his nerves. "Good thing we've already passed the ten-minute mark."

Aria rolled her eyes, brushing her dark curls away from her face. "Can we focus? We're here to investigate, not trade bad jokes."

"I thought my jokes were excellent," Zane quipped, but his grin faded as his gaze returned to the manor.

Theo shifted his grip on the relic in his hand—a small metallic object that glowed faintly. It was a family heirloom, passed down through generations, and was said to have protective powers. Its warmth was the only thing keeping the oppressive chill at bay. "Whatever's in there, we stick together. No wandering off, no splitting up. Agreed?"

Zane sighed dramatically. "Agreed, Captain Courage."

Aria shot Zane a look before stepping closer to Theo. "Do you really think the relic will work?" she asked softly.

Theo hesitated, feeling the weight of her question. "It's gotten us this far," he said finally. "Let's hope it's enough."

The Gate's Warning

The wrought-iron gate groaned in protest as Theo pushed it open. Strange symbols were carved into its rusted frame, their jagged edges glowing faintly in the dim light.

Aria crouched to inspect one of the symbols, her fingers hovering above the etched surface. "These match the ones from Amelia's journal. They're warnings, but... they also feel like invitations."

"Invitations to what?" Zane asked, leaning over her shoulder. "An early grave?"

Aria stood, brushing the dirt from her jeans. "Maybe. Or maybe something worse."

Theo stepped through the gate, his voice steady despite the tightness in his chest. "We'll find out soon enough. Let's go."

The Grand Foyer

The air inside the manor was cold and damp, heavy with the scent of rot and decay. Shadows stretched unnaturally along the walls, dancing in the faint beam of their flashlights.

Theo held the relic aloft, its glow illuminating the grand foyer. The remnants of a once-majestic staircase rose ahead, its banister splintered and draped in cobwebs. Above them, a chandelier hung precariously, its crystals dull with age.

"This place screams 'haunted,'" Zane said, his voice barely above a terrified whisper.

Aria shot him a wry look. "What gave it away? The creepy staircase or the fact that the shadows are moving?"

Zane smirked faintly. "Both."

Theo moved cautiously toward the center of the room, his flashlight scanning the walls. "Stay close. We don't know what's waiting for us."

The air grew colder as they moved deeper into the room. Zane's flashlight flickered, and for a moment, the beam caught something moving in the corner of the ceiling—a shadow that didn't belong to them.

"Did you see that?" Zane whispered, his voice tight.

Theo nodded, gripping the relic tighter. "Stay focused. We need to—"

A faint whisper echoed through the room, so soft it could have been the wind.

The First Chill

A sudden, bone-deep chill swept through the room, causing Theo to stop. The cold air fogged his breath, and the hair on the back of his neck stood on end.

"You okay?" Aria asked, stepping closer.

Theo nodded, though his voice was tight. "Yeah. Just... felt something."

Zane shivered, rubbing his arms. "Something like what? A ghost? A demon? Please tell me it wasn't a demon."

Before Theo could respond, the whisper came again—louder this time, more distinct. It sounded like his name, drawn out in a low, hissing breath.

"Theo..."

Theo froze, his heart pounding in his chest. The sound came from the shadows near the staircase, but nothing was there.

Aria glanced at him, her eyes wide. "What's wrong?"

"Nothing," he lied, his voice unconvincing. "Let's keep moving."

The Flickering Flashlight

As they moved toward the far side of the room, Zane's flashlight flickered again. This time, the beam cut out entirely, plunging them into darkness.

"What the—?!" Zane exclaimed, fumbling to turn his light back on.

Theo's and Aria's flashlights began to flicker. One by one, their beams faded, leaving only the faint glow of the relic to light the space.

The shadows seemed to grow in the dim light, stretching across the walls like living things. The whisper became louder now, and it wasn't alone this time.

Dozens of overlapping voices filled the room, their tones urgent and mocking.

"Leave..." "You don't belong here..." "Turn back..."

Theo's heart raced as he turned toward the mirror on the far wall. The relic's light reflected off its cracked surface, and for a moment, he thought he saw movement within.

The voices stopped abruptly, and the room fell silent.

Then, the figure appeared.

The Ghost in the Mirror

A pale, translucent face flickered into view in the mirror—a woman, her hollow eyes fixed on Theo. Her lips moved, forming words he couldn't hear.

Zane stumbled backward, nearly tripping over a broken chair. "What the hell is that?!"

Aria stepped closer, her flashlight shaking in her hand. "It's... her. Amelia."

The ghost's expression was pained, her mouth repeating the same word: Run.

A sudden wind surged through the room, extinguishing the relic's faint glow.

The figure in the mirror disappeared, leaving only darkness behind.

Cliffhanger

The flashlights sputtered back to life, their beams slicing through the shadows.

"What was that?" Zane asked, his voice shaking. "Please tell me someone else saw that."

Aria stared at the mirror, her face pale. "It wasn't just a trick. It was real."

Theo tightened his grip on the relic, his voice steady despite the fear coursing through him. "Whatever it was, it's trying to stop us. But we're not leaving until we figure this out."

The whispers returned, faint and insistent, as the three stood together, ready to face whatever lay ahead.

Chapter 2: The Forgotten Girl

The faint chill of Elmwood Manor followed Theo, Aria, and Zane as they moved cautiously through the labyrinth of darkened hallways. Each step echoed unnaturally, as though the manor itself was listening.

Aria led the way, the journal clutched tightly in her hands. "Amelia's room is upstairs," she said, her voice steady despite the tension in the air. "If what we saw in the foyer is any indication, the answers we're looking for are there."

Zane trailed behind, his flashlight sweeping over the peeling wallpaper and rotting furniture. "Sure. Let's head straight to the ghost's bedroom. Nothing bad could possibly happen there."

"Maybe something bad should happen," Aria shot back without turning around. "It's not like we're here to make friends."

Theo walked between them, the relic glowing faintly in his grip. "Both of you, focus. The whispers aren't gone—they're waiting for us to slip up."

As if on cue, the air grew colder, and a faint, disembodied giggle echoed through the corridor.

"I hate it here," Zane muttered.

Amelia's Room

The door to Amelia's room creaked open with a groan that sent chills up their spines. The room inside was eerily preserved, as though its occupant had left only moments ago. A small bed with a threadbare quilt sat against one wall, and a wooden toy chest rested at its foot.

But the mirror on the far wall caught Theo's attention. Its surface was cracked, and strange symbols were etched into its frame.

Aria stepped inside, her flashlight sweeping the room. "This is it," she whispered. "This is where she lived."

Zane leaned against the doorway, his expression wary. "She didn't live here. She was trapped here. Big difference."

Theo approached the mirror cautiously, the relic's glow reflecting off its jagged surface. He thought he saw movement within—briefly, a flicker of something pale and ghostly.

"Amelia?" he asked softly.

The mirror remained still, but the air around them grew heavier.

The Vision

Without warning, Theo was hit with a wave of vertigo. The room blurred, and he stumbled back, clutching the relic as images flooded his mind.

He saw a young girl—Amelia—standing in the corner of the room, her small hands gripping the mirror's edge. Her wide eyes were filled with fear as dark tendrils crept along the walls, wrapping around her ankles.

"Help me," her voice echoed faintly, distorted by the shadows that seemed to swallow her whole.

"Theo!" Aria's voice jolted him back to reality. She grabbed his arm, steadying him as he blinked away the vision.

"What happened?" she asked, her voice tinged with concern.

"I saw her," Theo said, his breath shaky. "She was... trapped. The Core had her even before it was fully formed."

Zane shifted uneasily. "That's not exactly comforting news. If the Core had that much power then, how much does it have now?"

Aria's brow furrowed as she opened the journal. "It doesn't matter. Whatever happened to Amelia started here. That means the answers are here, too."

The Journal's Secrets

Aria moved to the small desk beside the bed, its surface covered in dust. She opened the drawer, revealing an old, crumbling journal bound with faded leather.

"This must be hers," Aria said, carefully opening the book. The pages were filled with scrawled writing and crude drawings, many depicting the same symbols they had seen throughout the manor.

"Anything useful?" Zane asked, peering over her shoulder.

Aria scanned the pages, her eyes narrowing. "She wrote about the whispers. She called them... the voices of the veil. They started small, like faint echoes, but they grew stronger as the Core's power spread."

Theo leaned closer. "Does it say anything about how to stop it?"

Aria flipped to the final pages, her hands trembling slightly. "She mentions a place—something she called the Whispering Core. She wrote that it was the source of the veil's power. But she also wrote that she couldn't face it alone."

The Living Roots

Zane's flashlight flickered before they could examine the journal further, casting strange shadows across the room.

"Uh, guys?" he said, stepping back toward the door. "Tell me that's just the wind."

Theo and Aria turned to see what he was looking at. Dark roots had begun creeping through the cracks in the walls, their surfaces pulsing faintly with light.

"It's not the wind," Aria said, her voice tight.

The roots twisted and writhed, growing longer with each passing second. They snaked toward the mirror, their tips glowing as they pressed against its surface.

"The mirror," Theo said, raising the relic. "It's connected to the Core. It's feeding on the room."

The whispers surged, overlapping into a chaotic storm of voices. The mirror began to glow, its surface rippling like water.

The Whispers Overwhelm

The room erupted in chaos. The roots lashed out violently, knocking over furniture and smashing the toy chest to splinters. The whispers grew louder, filling the trio's ears with overlapping cries and taunts.

"You can't stop it." "You'll fail." "Leave while you can."

Aria clutched the journal to her chest, her voice rising above the chaos. "Theo! The relic!"

Theo stepped forward, the relic blazing in his hand. The light cut through the shadows, forcing the roots to recoil.

"Get out of here!" he shouted.

Aria and Zane hesitated, their eyes darting between Theo and the mirror.

"Now!" Theo barked, his voice leaving no room for argument.

The Journal's Warning

They scrambled out of the room just as the mirror shattered, sending a shockwave through the hallway. The whispers were abruptly silenced, leaving only the sound of their ragged breathing.

Aria clutched the journal tightly, her eyes wide. "That wasn't just the veil. That was the Core itself."

Theo leaned against the wall, his chest heaving. "It knows we're trying to stop it. And it won't let us get any closer without a fight."

Zane looked back toward the room, now silent and still. "So what do we do now?"

Aria opened the journal, her fingers brushing over Amelia's final entry. "We find the Whispering Core. And we finish what she started."

Cliffhanger

The whispers began to stir again, faint and insistent, as the faint glow of the roots returned in the distance.

Theo gripped the relic, its light flickering as he stared down the darkened hallway. "We keep moving," he said, his voice steady. "And we don't look back."

Chapter 3: A Town in Decline

The morning light did little to warm Elmwood. The town was shrouded in an unnatural stillness, its streets eerily empty and its buildings weathered by time and neglect. Theo, Aria, and Zane stood in the square, the relic faintly glowing in Theo's hand.

"This doesn't feel right," Theo said, his voice low. The relic pulsed weakly, as though it, too, were affected by the oppressive silence. "It's like the veil is still clinging to this place."

Aria nodded, flipping through Amelia's journal. "The whispers may have left the manor, but the Core's reach is deeper than we thought. The town is part of its web—it's been feeding off these people for decades."

Zane glanced around, his grip tightening on his flashlight. "Great. So, the whole town's been living in creepy, spooky hypnosis? Fantastic. What's next, possessed librarians?"

"Stay focused," Theo said, scanning the empty streets. "The journal mentioned symbols in the town. If we can find them, we might figure out how the Core spread its influence—and how to stop it for good."

"The library's probably our best bet," Aria suggested, gesturing to the weathered brick building at the far end of the square. "If anyone kept records of the town's history, they'll be there."

Zane sighed, his flashlight sweeping over the crumbling storefronts. "Of course, it's the library. Why couldn't it be a diner with pancakes instead?"

The Reluctant Librarian

The library's interior was dim and musty, and the faint scent of aged paper filled the air. Rows of shelves stood like silent sentinels, their spines coated in a fine layer of dust.

At the counter sat an older man with a hunched back and deep-set eyes. He looked up as they entered, his expression one of immediate suspicion.

"We're closed," he said gruffly, returning to a stack of crumbling newspapers.

"We're not here to borrow books," Theo said, stepping forward. "We're looking for information about Elmwood's history—specifically, anything about the manor or the Whisperveil Society."

The man froze, his eyes darting toward the relic in Theo's hand. His voice dropped to a whisper. "You shouldn't be asking about that. It's not safe."

Aria pulled Amelia's journal from her bag and placed it on the counter. "We've already been inside the manor. We've destroyed three anchors, and we're working to weaken the Core. But we need to understand how it all started."

The man's face paled, and he leaned closer, his voice trembling. "You've broken the anchors? Then you've drawn its attention. The Core doesn't let go easily."

"That's why we're here," Theo said firmly. "If you know anything, tell us."

After a moment of hesitation, the man gestured for them to follow.

The Secret Archives

The librarian led them to a back room, its door secured with a rusted padlock. He fumbled with the key, glancing over his shoulder nervously.

"This town has a long history," he said as the lock clicked open. "Most of it's been forgotten—or buried on purpose."

The room was cluttered with faded maps, handwritten journals, and yellowed photographs. Aria's eyes widened as she took it all in.

"This is incredible," she said, carefully picking up a leather-bound journal. "Some of these records are from the Whisperveil Society itself."

The librarian nodded grimly. "They started out trying to protect us. They thought they could contain the Core's power and keep it from spreading. But they underestimated its hunger."

Theo scanned the shelves, his fingers brushing over the spines of books. "What happened to them?"

"They fed the Core," the librarian said, his voice heavy. "They sacrificed their fears and regrets to keep it sated. But it was never enough. The more they gave, the stronger it became."

Aria turned the pages of a journal, her brow furrowing. "These symbols—they aren't just warnings. They're anchors. There are more anchors hidden here in the town."

The librarian nodded. "At least three. Destroying them won't be easy. The echoes will fight to protect them."

The Anchor in the Library

The relic in Theo's hand pulsed faintly as they returned to the main room. The whispers began to stir, faint and insistent, as if the library itself were alive.

"This is it," Theo said, his voice steady. "The anchor's here somewhere."

Aria scanned the shelves, her flashlight sweeping over the rows of books. "It's not just anywhere. The symbols point to the foundation."

Theo turned toward the librarian. "Is there a basement?"

The man hesitated, then nodded. "There's a trapdoor under the far shelf. Be careful. Once you disturb the anchor, it'll fight back."

The Fight for the Anchor

The trapdoor creaked open, revealing a narrow staircase leading into darkness. The air grew colder with each step.

At the bottom, they found a small stone chamber. In the center stood a pedestal, its surface etched with glowing runes. Atop it rested a shard of blackened glass, pulsing faintly with light.

"This is it," Aria said, clutching the journal.

Theo stepped forward, raising the relic. The whispers surged, and the shadows on the walls came to life, twisting into humanoid forms with glowing, hollow eyes.

One of the shadows lunged at Zane, its claws slicing through the air. He swung his hatchet, cutting through its form, but it reformed instantly, hissing as it lunged again.

"They're protecting the anchor!" Aria shouted, opening the journal. "I'll start the incantation— just keep them off me!"

Theo held the relic high, its light flaring brightly and forcing the shadows to retreat. "We'll hold them back. Just hurry!"

The chamber trembled as Aria chanted the incantation, her voice steady despite the chaos. The runes on the pedestal flared brighter, and the whispers became a deafening roar.

One of the shadows lunged at her, but Theo stepped between them, the relic's light slicing through the figure. Zane swung his hatchet wildly, carving through the shadows as they closed in.

"Almost there!" Aria shouted.

The shard atop the pedestal began to crack, and the chamber trembled violently. Aria finished the ritual with a final chant, and the pedestal shattered, sending a shockwave through the room.

The shadows let out a collective wail before dissolving into mist, and the whispers fell silent.

Aftermath

Theo helped Aria to her feet, the journal still clutched tightly in her hands.

"That's one more anchor down," he said, his voice firm.

Zane leaned against the wall, catching his breath. "How many more of these things are there?"

Aria opened the journal, her brow furrowed. "Two, maybe three. But if this one fought this hard to stay intact, the others will be worse."

Theo nodded, the relic still warm in his hand. "Then we keep going. We're not stopping until the Core is gone."

Cliffhanger

As they climbed back up the narrow staircase to the library's main floor, the whispers stirred again—faint but sharper now.

"You think you are winning..."

The words echoed through the air, clear and taunting. The librarian stood by the counter, his face pale as he pointed toward the window.

Outside, the streets of Elmwood were no longer empty. Shadows shifted along the sidewalks, moving in unnatural, jerking motions. In the distance, faint ember-like eyes peered out from the darkened alleys.

"The echoes," Theo whispered, gripping the relic tightly.

Zane swallowed hard. "Looks like they're not happy about us breaking that anchor."

Aria's voice was steady, though her hands trembled as she held the journal. "Then we better move fast because they're coming."

The whispers swelled, overlapping in a chaotic symphony as the glowing eyes grew closer, and the trio realized Elmwood wasn't as quiet as they had thought.

Chapter 4: Into the Whispering Depths

The trio stood in the manor's decaying foyer, the quiet oppressive as they steeled themselves for the descent into the basement. The faint glow of the relic cast long shadows on the walls, and the whispers, though distant, grew louder with every passing second.

"This is where Amelia's journal says the Nexus is," Aria said, her flashlight shaking slightly as she pointed toward the heavy wooden door at the far end of the hall. "The Core's heart, buried beneath the house."

Zane glanced at the door, then back at Theo. "And we're just going to march straight in, huh? No prep, no backup? Sounds solid."

Theo shot him a look, the relic pulsing faintly in his grip. "We don't have time for backup. The Core knows we're coming. If we wait, it'll only get stronger."

Zane sighed, gripping his hatchet tightly. "Fine. But if a creepy root monster grabs me, I blame you."

Aria stepped forward, her voice steady despite the tension in her shoulders. "Let's just make sure we're the ones walking out of here, okay?"

Theo nodded, pushing open the door.

The Descent

The stairs into the basement were steep and narrow, the air growing colder with every step. The glow of the relic lit the way, casting faint light on the damp stone walls.

Aria clutched Amelia's journal, tracing the runes on its cover. "The closer we get, the more active the whispers will become. The Core uses them to disorient us, to make us turn on each other."

"Great," Zane muttered. "So not only do we have to fight shadow monsters, but we might also end up fighting each other. This keeps getting better."

Theo paused on the stairs, his voice firm. "That's not going to happen. Whatever the whispers show us, we focus. We trust each other. That's how we win."

Aria gave him a slight, determined nod. Zane rolled his eyes but fell silent, his grip tightening on his hatchet.

The whispers began to stir, faint and insistent, as though testing their resolve.

The Whispering Chamber

At the bottom of the stairs, the trio entered a vast chamber. The walls were lined with twisting roots that pulsed faintly with light, and the air was thick with the sound of overlapping voices. An ancient door stood in the center of the room, its surface covered in glowing runes that shifted and writhed like living things.

"That's it," Aria whispered, her gaze fixed on the door. "The Nexus."

Theo stepped forward, the relic's light flaring brighter as he approached. The voices were no longer whispers, their tones shifting from faint murmurs to mocking laughter.

"You can't stop us." "You're too late." "Turn back or be consumed."

Zane swung his flashlight toward the walls, his breath catching as the shadows rippled and moved. "I really hate this place."

Aria opened the journal, scanning the pages frantically. "There's a ritual to weaken the Nexus—if I can just... find it..."

The roots along the walls began to shift, their movements slow but deliberate as they snaked toward the trio.

"Whatever you're going to do, do it fast," Theo said, his voice tense.

The Core's Defense

The roots lashed out suddenly, their tendrils wrapping around Zane's ankle and pulling him to the ground.

"Zane!" Aria shouted, dropping the journal as she rushed to help him.

"I'm fine!" Zane yelled, swinging his hatchet wildly. The blade sliced through the root, which recoiled with a hiss.

Theo raised the relic, its light flaring brightly. The roots pulled back, retreating into the walls.

"You cannot win." "This is our world." "You will be consumed."

Aria grabbed the journal, her hands shaking as she flipped to the ritual. "Theo, keep them back! I need a few more seconds!"

The roots surged forward, faster this time, their glowing tendrils reaching for the trio. Theo stepped between them, the relic blazing as he forced the roots to recoil again.

"Zane, cover her!" Theo shouted, swinging the relic toward a massive root that lunged for Aria.

Zane nodded, positioning himself between Aria and the walls. "You heard the man. Hands off the book!"

The Ancient Door

As Aria began the incantation, the runes on the ancient door glowed more intensely. The whispers shifted, their tones becoming desperate and pleading.

"Stop!" "You don't understand!" "We are eternal!"

The chamber trembled, dust and debris falling from the ceiling as the roots writhed violently. The door itself pulsed with energy, the runes flickering as though trying to resist the ritual.

Theo's grip on the relic tightened, his voice calm. "Don't listen to them. They're just trying to scare us."

Aria's voice rose above the chaos, her chanting growing louder and more confident. The runes on the door began to crack, light spilling from the fractures.

The roots let out a deafening wail, their tendrils retreating into the walls as the door began to splinter.

"Almost there!" Aria shouted, her voice triumphant.

The Ominous Warning

The door broke apart with a final, shattering crack, and energy surged through the chamber, knocking the trio off their feet. The whispers fell silent, leaving only the sound of their ragged breathing.

Aria sat up, clutching the journal tightly. "We did it," she said, her voice relieved.

Theo helped her to her feet, his gaze fixed on the now-open doorway. Beyond it lay a dark tunnel, its walls pulsing faintly with light.

"We're not done yet," he said, his voice low. "The Core's still ahead."

Zane groaned, leaning against the wall as he caught his breath. "Of course it is. Because why would anything about this be easy?"

Aria glanced at the tunnel, her expression somber. "Amelia couldn't face the Core alone. But she didn't have us."

Theo nodded, gripping the relic tightly. "Then let's finish this."

Cliffhanger

As they stepped toward the tunnel, the whispers returned, faint and distant, as though echoing from the very heart of the veil.

"You are not ready." "This will be your end."

The light from the relic sparkled, casting long shadows as the trio disappeared into the darkness.

Chapter 5: The Whispering Core

The ancient tunnel was a void of shifting shadows and pulsing light. Its walls seemed alive, twisting with dark roots that moved as if sensing the trio's presence. The whispers surrounded them, overlapping and chaotic, growing louder with every step.

"You cannot survive this." "Turn back or be consumed." "We are eternal."

Theo held the relic tightly, its light steady but dim against the oppressive darkness. "Keep moving," he said, his voice firm despite the knot of fear tightening in his chest.

Aria clutched Amelia's journal, her eyes scanning the runes that glowed faintly along the tunnel walls. "The Core is close. The whispers are strongest here."

Zane swung his flashlight toward the shifting shadows, his grip tightening on his hatchet. "Yeah, I can tell. Every creepy voice in this place is having a party in my ears."

Theo glanced back at him. "Just focus. They're trying to mess with us."

Zane smirked faintly, though his tension was evident. "Oh, don't worry, Captain Courage. I'm perfectly fine in this nightmare cave of doom."

Aria gave him a sideways glance. "Let's hope your sarcasm is as sharp as that hatchet."

The Core Revealed

The tunnel opened into a massive chamber, its size impossible to reconcile with the manor above. The ceiling was lost in darkness, and the floor was a web of glowing roots that pulsed like veins, their light converging at the center of the room.

There, suspended in midair, was the Whispering Core.

The Core was a sphere of liquid-like light and shadow, its surface rippling with distorted faces and shifting symbols. It pulsed with a rhythm that seemed to echo in their chests, like the beating of an otherworldly heart.

Theo took a step forward, the relic flaring slightly in his hand. The whispers swelled, their tones shifting from taunting to furious.

"You cannot destroy us." "We are your fear. Your regret. Your truth."

Aria's voice was barely above a whisper. "This is it. The heart of the veil."

Zane stared at the Core, his usual bravado fading. "Yeah, and it's way worse than I imagined. How do we even fight that?"

The Core's First Attack

Before Theo could answer, the Core shuddered violently, and tendrils of shadow erupted from its surface, lashing out toward the trio.

"Move!" Theo shouted, raising the relic as one of the tendrils shot toward him. The light from the relic glowed, forcing the tendril to recoil with a screech.

Zane swung his hatchet at another tendril, severing it, but the piece dissolved and reformed almost instantly. "It's regenerating!" he yelled, dodging another attack.

Aria flipped through the journal frantically, her fingers trembling. "The Core feeds on fear and doubt! We have to disrupt its connection to us!"

Theo held the relic high, its light creating a temporary barrier against the tendrils. "How?"

Aria scanned the pages, her voice shaking. "The journal mentions a ritual, but it requires all three of us to focus. If we can distract it long enough—"

"No pressure," Zane muttered, deflecting another tendril with his hatchet.

Facing Their Fears

The Core's surface shifted, and its faces became more apparent. One by one, they transformed into reflections of the trio—distorted and twisted, their expressions filled with anguish and fear.

Theo froze as his face stared back at him from the Core, its eyes hollow.

"You failed her," the Core whispered, its voice taking on an eerie version of his own. "You let her slip away. And you will fail again."

The relic trembled in his hand as doubt surged through him.

Aria's voice broke through the haze. "Theo! Don't let it in!"

She turned back to the journal, but her image appeared in the Core, its voice taunting her. "You think knowledge will protect you? You couldn't even save your parents. You're nothing without your books."

Her hands shook, but she kept reading, her voice rising above the whispers. "You're wrong," she muttered, her tone defiant.

Zane staggered back as the Core's tendrils shifted, forming the image of his father lying in a hospital bed. The figure's lips moved, mouthing words only Zane could hear.

"No," Zane said, his voice cracking. "You're not real. You're not real!"

The Ritual

"Theo!" Aria shouted, holding up the journal. "The relic needs all of us! We must focus together—on what makes us stronger, not weaker!"

Theo snapped out of his daze, his grip on the relic tightening. He stepped toward the Core, its tendrils lashing out but unable to penetrate the light. "We can do this. Together."

Aria joined him, her voice steady as she began chanting the words from the journal. The runes on the floor began to glow, their light pushing back the shadows.

Zane hesitated, his gaze fixed on the image of his father. Then, with a deep breath, he raised his hatchet and stepped forward. "I'm with you."

The Core shuddered violently, its surface cracking as the light from the relic grew brighter.

The Core Weakens

The whispers became screams as the trio's combined energy disrupted the Core's hold on the chamber. The tendrils recoiled, and the distorted faces within the Core began to dissolve.

"You cannot sever us!" the Core roared, shaking the chamber. "We are eternal!"

Theo took another step forward, the relic blazing in his hand. "You're not eternal. You're just afraid. And fear can be beaten."

Aria's chanting grew louder, the runes flaring brightly as cracks spread across the Core's surface.

Zane swung his hatchet at a tendril, his voice rising over the chaos. "You heard him! Time to finish this!"

The Core let out a deafening wail as the cracks deepened, light spilling from within.

Cliffhanger

Just as the Core seemed on the verge of collapse, the chamber trembled violently. The roots along the walls began to glow, their light pulsing in rhythm with the Core's shuddering energy.

"Theo!" Aria shouted, her voice panicked. "The Core—it's not breaking! It's—"

The relic's glow surged, throwing light across the chamber in a blinding pulse erupting from the Core, engulfing the trio.

For a moment, there was nothing but silence.

Then, as the light faded, Theo opened his eyes to find himself alone in the chamber. The Core was still there, its cracks glowing faintly as it slowly began to mend.

"Theo..." a voice whispered, faint and chilling.

He turned, his heart pounding, but the room was empty.

Chapter 6: The Keeper's Warning

The silence was suffocating. Theo stood alone in the cavernous chamber, the Core looming before him like a pulsating wound in reality. Its surface shimmered faintly, the cracks from their assault glowing with a dim, malevolent light as they began to seal.

"Aria? Zane?" Theo called, his voice echoing into the void.

There was no answer. The whispers, which had grown silent in the wake of the Core's eruption, now stirred faintly, a low murmur rising from the walls.

"You cannot save them," the whispers hissed, overlapping in a haunting melody. "They are ours now."

Theo's grip tightened on the relic, its glow weak but persistent. "You're lying," he said, his voice steady despite the dread curling in his chest.

The whispers laughed, mocking and hollow. "Am I?"

The Keeper Appears

A faint light flickered at the edge of the chamber, drawing Theo's attention. He turned, his heart pounding, as a figure materialized from the shadows.

It was the Keeper.

The spectral figure was draped in tattered robes, its face obscured beneath a hood that seemed to shift like mist. Its hollow eyes glowed faintly, fixed on Theo with an unblinking intensity.

"You have come farther than most," the Keeper said, its voice a low, resonant echo. "And yet, you are still unprepared."

Theo instinctively raised the relic, its light flaring weakly in response. "What do you mean? Where are my friends?"

The Keeper tilted its head slightly as though studying him. "Your friends are lost between worlds, caught in the wake of the Core's defense. Their survival depends on your choices now."

Theo took a step forward, his jaw tightening. "Then tell me what I need to do to save them."

The Warning

The Keeper's gaze shifted to the Core, its form shimmering as though struggling to remain tethered to the space. "The Core is not a singular entity," it said. "It is the culmination of fear, regret, and despair—an endless cycle that feeds on those who cannot face their truths."

"We broke the anchors," Theo said, his voice firm. "We weakened it. Why isn't it gone?"

The Keeper raised a skeletal hand, gesturing to the fractured surface of the Core. "You attacked its form but not its essence. The Core cannot be destroyed by force alone. To sever its hold, you must face the truth it holds over you."

Theo's chest tightened, the whisper now louder swirled around him like a cold wind. "What truth?"

The Keeper's gaze bore into him. "The truth of your own fear. Only by confronting it will you unlock the strength to shatter the veil."

A Glimpse of the Truth

The Core pulsed violently, and the chamber trembled. Images flickered around Theo like shards of broken glass reflecting his memories.

He saw Amelia, her small hands gripping the mirror's edge in her room, her wide eyes filled with fear. Her voice echoed faintly: "Help me..."

The memory shifted, and Theo saw himself standing outside the manor's gates, hesitating as Aria and Zane urged him forward. The weight of his doubt was palpable, a crushing force that rooted him in place.

"You carry the fear of failure," the Keeper said, its voice cutting through the chaos. "It binds you to the Core as surely as its tendrils bind this house."

Theo clenched his fists, the relic pulsing in his hand. "I'm not afraid of failing. I'm afraid of letting them down."

"And that fear gives the Core its power over you," the Keeper said. "Only by releasing it can you hope to free your friends—and yourself."

The Keeper's Gift

The Keeper extended its hand, and a small, glowing object appeared between them. It was a shard of light, shimmering like a piece of a star.

"This is the Keeper's Aegis," it said. "A fragment of the light that once sealed the veil. It will guide you, but only if you wield it without doubt."

Theo reached for the shard, its warmth spreading as his fingers closed around it. The whispers recoiled, their tones shifting from mocking to furious.

"You cannot trust him." "He will fail you." "The veil is eternal!"

The Keeper stepped back, its form beginning to fade. "The path ahead will test you, Theo. You must decide whether to face the Core's truth—or become part of its cycle."

The Return of His Friends

As the Keeper vanished, the chamber pulsed with light, and Theo staggered back as Aria and Zane materialized beside him.

Aria gasped, clutching the journal tightly. "What just happened? We were... I don't even know where we were."

Zane shook his head, his eyes wide. "Pretty sure I was nowhere, and let me tell you, it's not great."

Theo stepped between them, holding up the shard of light. "The Keeper gave us this. It's called the Aegis. It's the only thing strong enough to sever the Core's hold."

Aria's eyes widened as she examined the glowing shard. "This is the light Amelia wrote about— the one that can break the veil."

Zane stared at the Core, his grip tightening on his hatchet. "So, what's the plan? Because that thing doesn't look like it will let us walk up and stab it."

Cliffhanger

The chamber trembled again, and the Core began to pulse more violently, its cracks sealing faster than before. The whispers surged, their tones desperate and furious.

"You cannot win." "You cannot escape." "The veil will consume you."

Theo turned to his friends, his steady voice. "We don't let it. We use the Aegis, and we finish this."

The light from the shard flared as they stepped toward the Core, the whispers rising to a deafening roar.

Chapter 7: Fractured Realities

The chamber trembled violently as the trio advanced toward the Core, the Keeper's Aegis glowing brightly in Theo's hand. The whispers had risen to a deafening roar, their tones fractured and desperate.

"You cannot sever us." "We are endless." "Fear cannot be destroyed."

Theo glanced at Aria and Zane, their faces pale but resolute. "Stay close," he said. "The Core knows we're coming. It'll try to throw everything it has at us."

Aria nodded, clutching Amelia's journal. "The Keeper said the Veil feeds on fear and doubt. Whatever happens, we can't let it into our heads."

Zane smirked faintly, gripping his hatchet. "Easy for you to say, Ms. Encyclopedia. I'm sure this place reads my mind like an open book."

The Core pulsed again, and the room became a kaleidoscope of shifting images and shadows.

A Fractured Reality

The ground beneath them vanished, replaced by an endless void of twisting pathways. The trio stood on a narrow, jagged platform suspended in the air, with countless other paths spiraling off.

Theo staggered as the platform shifted beneath his feet. "What is this?"

Aria scanned the surroundings, her voice tight. "The Veil. It's warping reality around us."

Zane swung his flashlight toward the void, his breath catching as flickering images began to form. "Uh, guys? I think it's about to get worse."

The images coalesced into haunting scenes: a darkened room filled with shadowy figures, a graveyard lit by flickering lanterns, and a forest consumed by glowing roots. The whispers became distinct voices, each cutting through the chaos with chilling clarity.

Theo's Fear

Theo's surroundings blurred, and suddenly, he was back in the manor's foyer. The air was thick with dust and decay, and the whispers had quieted into a single, chilling voice.

"You failed her, Theo."

He turned, his heart pounding as Amelia's ghostly form appeared at the edge of the room. She stared at him with wide, accusing eyes, her small hands gripping the mirror's edge.

"You left me," she whispered, her voice trembling. "You said you'd help, but you didn't. You let me fall."

"No," Theo said, his voice cracking. "I didn't—I couldn't save you. I tried."

The mirror shattered, and the shards swirled around him, each reflecting his face, distorted and filled with anguish.

"Do you think you'll save them?" the voice hissed. "You couldn't even save me."

Aria's Fear

Aria blinked, and the jagged platform beneath her feet dissolved into the familiar surroundings of her childhood home. She stood in her parents' study, the shelves lined with books she hadn't touched in years.

A figure sat at the desk, its face obscured by shadows. It turned toward her slowly, its voice cold and cutting.

"You think knowledge will save you?" the figure asked. "You couldn't even save us."

The room filled with smoke, and Aria coughed as the walls around her began to burn. She stumbled back, her hands trembling as the journal slipped from her grasp.

"You hide behind your books, but they won't protect you," the voice said. "You're alone, Aria. You've always been alone."

Zane's Fear

Zane stood in a hospital room, the fluorescent lights flickering faintly. He recognized the bed instantly, his stomach twisting as he saw his father lying motionless beneath the thin sheets.

"No," Zane whispered, taking a step back. "This isn't real."

The figure in the bed sat up slowly, its eyes hollow and lifeless. "Why did you leave me?" it asked, its voice rasping. "You let me die alone."

Zane shook his head, gripping his hatchet tightly. "You're not him. You're not real."

The figure stood, its form twisting and warping into a monstrous silhouette. "But I am your truth," it said, echoing.

Breaking the Illusions

Theo raised the Aegis, its light flaring brightly as he fought to push past the whispers. "This isn't real," he said. "You're just trying to stop me."

The mirror fragments dissolved, and the manor's foyer blurred into darkness. Theo found himself back on the jagged platform, the Aegis glowing brightly in his hand.

"Aria! Zane!" he shouted, his voice echoing into the void.

Aria's surroundings flickered, and she clung to Theo's voice. "It's not real," she whispered, her hands trembling as she reached for the journal. "They're just trying to make me afraid."

The burning study dissolved, and she stumbled back onto the platform, gasping as she clutched the journal tightly.

Zane swung his hatchet at the monstrous figure, his voice rising above the whispers. "I'm not afraid of you!" he shouted. "You're not real!"

The hospital room shattered like glass, and Zane reappeared on the platform, breathing heavily but steady.

Reuniting

The trio stood together, the Aegis glowing brightly between them. The whispers grew even louder, but their tones were no longer mocking or taunting—they were desperate.

"You cannot resist us." "We are eternal."

Theo turned to his friends, his voice firm. "We're not alone. Whatever the Core throws at us, we face it together."

Aria nodded, her grip on the journal steady. "It can't beat all of us. Not if we stand as one."

Zane smirked, lifting his hatchet. "Let's show it what happens when it messes with the wrong people."

The Aegis flared, its light spreading across the platform as the trio stepped forward. The fractured reality around them began to crack and dissolve, revealing the Core's chamber again.

Cliffhanger

As the chamber returned to focus, the Core loomed before them, its surface glowing with a sickly, pulsing light. The cracks they had inflicted earlier were nearly gone, and its tendrils lashed out violently, shattering the walls.

The whispers returned, louder and more chaotic than ever.

"You will not escape." "This is where it ends."

Theo gripped the Aegis tightly, forcing calm into his voice. "You're right about one thing. This is where it ends—for you."

The chamber trembled as the trio advanced toward the Core, the light of the Aegis blazing
brighter than ever.

Chapter 8: Ghosts of the Past

The air felt heavier as the trio stepped cautiously onto the manor's upper floors. The broken walls and crumbling wood seemed to groan with each step, as if the house itself were alive. The faint glow of the relic in Theo's hand barely penetrated the oppressive darkness.

"Why do I feel like we're walking into a giant trap?" Zane muttered, swinging his flashlight toward the shadows that shifted along the corridor.

"Because we probably are," Aria replied, clutching Amelia's journal tightly. "The Core knows we're getting closer. It'll try to stop us by any means possible."

Theo paused, scanning the corridor. Faded portraits lined the walls, their subjects long forgotten. Dust and cobwebs clung to every surface, but the whispering voices were more distinct here—almost mournful.

"Listen," Theo said, his voice low.

The trio stopped, and the whispers became audible, forming fragmented words.

"Why did you leave?" "Save us..." "Don't let it win."

Zane shuddered. "This place just keeps getting creepier."

The Portrait of Amelia

As they continued, Theo's light fell on a large, ornate portrait at the end of the corridor. It depicted a young girl with braided hair standing in a sunlit garden, her expression a mix of joy and melancholy.

"Amelia," Aria whispered, stepping closer.

The light from the relic reflected off the painting, and for a moment, the girl's eyes seemed to follow Theo. A faint shiver ran down his spine as the whispers shifted, their tone pleading.

"She's been trapped in this house for so long," Aria said softly. "It's like she's still trying to reach out to us."

Theo nodded, his jaw tightening. "We're not leaving until we set her free."

The air around them grew colder, and the whispers turned into faint laughter that echoed down the corridor.

The Children's Room

The laughter led them to a small door at the end of the hall. Zane pushed it open cautiously, revealing a room filled with decaying toys and broken furniture. A faint glow emanated from a pile of blocks in the corner.

"This is... unsettling," Zane muttered, stepping inside.

Aria knelt near the blocks, brushing away the dust. The light revealed small carvings on the wooden surfaces—symbols similar to those in the journal.

"These were hers," she said, her voice tinged with sadness. "She was just a child when the Core took her."

Theo approached a rocking chair near the window, its surface warped and splintered with age. As he reached out, the chair began to move on its own, creaking slowly back and forth.

The laughter grew louder, and the temperature in the room plummeted.

"We're not alone," Theo said, gripping the relic tightly.

Amelia's Ghost

A faint figure began to materialize in the center of the room. Amelia's translucent form shimmered like a mirage, her braids glowing faintly in the dim light. Her eyes were wide, her expression one of sorrow and fear.

"Amelia," Aria said softly, rising to her feet.

The ghost turned toward them, her lips moving silently. The room momentarily fell silent, as if the house was holding its breath.

Then her voice broke through, faint and trembling. "Help me..."

Theo stepped forward, the relic pulsing in his hand. "We're here to help," he said. "We're going to free you from this place."

Amelia's gaze shifted to the relic, and a flicker of hope crossed her face. "The Core..." she whispered. "It won't let me go. It won't let any of us go."

The room trembled, and the shadows on the walls began to twist and writhe.

Shared Visions

Before anyone could react, a surge of energy erupted from Amelia's ghost, enveloping the trio in a blinding light.

Theo blinked as the world around him dissolved into a vivid vision. He saw Amelia as a child, running through a sunlit garden, her laughter ringing out. But the scene darkened, the garden fading into a desolate landscape as roots began to creep toward her.

She screamed, and the roots ensnared her, pulling her toward the Core's pulsating heart.

Aria's vision was different. She stood in Amelia's room, watching as the girl frantically carved symbols into her toys and walls, tears streaming down her face. The whispers were deafening, drowning out her cries for help.

Zane found himself in the foyer, watching Amelia's parents arguing in hushed voices. "The Core will consume us all," her father said, his voice trembling. "We have to leave her. It's the only way to save ourselves."

"No!" Amelia's mother shouted, but the scene shifted, and Zane saw the family's belongings abandoned as they fled the manor, leaving the girl behind.

Breaking the Vision

The visions faded, and the trio returned to the children's room. Amelia's ghost flickered, her form trembling as the shadows in the room grew more aggressive.

"She's showing us the truth," Aria said, her voice shaky. "Her family left her. They thought it would save them, but it fed the Core."

Theo gripped the relic tightly. "Then we finish what her family couldn't. We end this."

Amelia's ghost pointed toward a small chest in the corner of the room. "The key," she whispered. "You'll need it."

Theo approached the chest, the relic's light revealing an ornate key carved with intricate symbols. The moment he touched it, the room erupted in chaos.

The Core's Retaliation

The shadows lashed out, their tendrils slamming into the walls and shattering the toys across the floor. The laughter turned into furious shrieks, and the temperature in the room plummeted.

"Get back!" Theo shouted, raising the relic. Its light flared, forcing the shadows to recoil, but they regrouped quickly, their attacks growing more frenzied.

Aria clutched the journal, flipping to a page filled with protective runes. "These symbols—if I can draw them, they'll hold off the shadows!"

"Do it fast!" Zane yelled, swinging his hatchet at a tendril that lunged toward him.

Aria knelt on the floor, using a piece of broken chalk to trace the runes. The sounded mocked and taunted her with every stroke.

"You can't save her." "You'll fail like the rest."

"Shut up!" Aria snapped, her hand steady as she completed the final symbol.

The runes flared, creating a barrier of light around the trio. The shadows screamed, retreating into the walls as the room fell silent again.

Cliffhanger

Theo held the key tightly, his breath ragged. Amelia's ghost flickered, her expression a mix of relief and sadness.

"Thank you," she whispered. "But the Core is waiting. It knows you're coming."

Before Theo could respond, her form dissolved into light, leaving the room in silence.

Aria stood, brushing dust from her knees. "The key must unlock something in the Nexus," she said.

"Or another trap," Zane muttered, leaning on his hatchet. "Either way, it's not like we have a choice."

Theo glanced at the door, his grip tightening on the relic. "Then let's go. It's time to face the Core."

The trio stepped into the hallway, the whispers stirring once more as they made their way toward the Nexus.

Chapter 9: A Test of Courage

The whispers swelled as the trio descended deeper into the heart of Elmwood Manor. The ancient staircase creaked beneath their feet, each step bringing them closer to the Nexus. Amelia had given them the ornate key, which hung on a cord around Theo's neck, its surface faintly glowing with the same light as the relic in his hand.

"We're getting close," Aria said, her voice steady but laced with tension. "The Core knows we have the key. It's not going to let us walk in."

"Wouldn't be the first time," Zane muttered, gripping his hatchet tightly. "Let's just hope this doesn't throw another freaky shadow tantrum."

Theo paused, scanning the dim corridor ahead. The air was thick, almost suffocating, and the walls seemed to pulse faintly with light, like veins carrying some unholy lifeblood. "We've dealt with worse," he said, his voice firm. "Whatever it throws at us, we'll handle it. Together."

The words hung in the air as they reached the bottom of the staircase, where an ancient door stood waiting. Its surface was carved with intricate runes that glowed faintly, shifting and writhing like living things.

Theo lifted the key, its light flaring as it neared the lock.

The Door to the Nexus

The key touched the lock, and the runes on the door blazed to life. The whispers rose into a deafening roar, and the ground beneath them trembled.

"You think you are brave." "You are nothing but fear." "Turn back or be consumed."

Theo clenched his jaw, forcing the key into the lock and turning it. The runes flared, and the door swung open with a low, guttural groan, revealing a cavernous chamber beyond.

The Nexus was vast, its walls lined with twisting roots that pulsed with an ominous red light. At the center of the room, suspended above a pool of shifting shadows, was the Core.

It was more prominent now, its surface alive with writhing tendrils and distorted faces that screamed silently as they twisted and shifted. The whispers emanating from it were overwhelming, filling the chamber with a sense of dread so powerful it made the air hard to breathe.

The Test Begins

As the trio stepped inside, the door slammed shut behind them, cutting off their escape. The relic in Theo's hand flared brightly, pushing back the encroaching darkness, but the Core's presence was suffocating.

"It's stronger," Aria said, her voice trembling. She clutched the journal tightly, her knuckles white. "The closer we get, the more it's feeding off us."

Zane swung his flashlight toward the shadows that writhed along the walls. "So, what's the plan? Because I'm not seeing a lot of options here."

Theo stepped forward, the relic glowing brighter in his hand. "We hold our ground. Aria, find whatever ritual we need to finish this. Zane and I will keep it off you."

Before anyone could respond, the Core shuddered violently, and a surge of energy erupted, sending the trio sprawling.

Facing Their Fears

The chamber twisted around them, and Theo found himself alone, the relic's glow flickering weakly. The whispers grew sharper, each cutting into his mind like a blade.

"You can't save them." "They will fall because of you." "Amelia's fate will be theirs."

Images flashed before him: Zane engulfed by shadowy tendrils, Aria consumed by the Core's light, Amelia's pleading face as the mirror shattered around her.

"No!" Theo shouted, gripping the relic tightly. "You don't control me!"

The relic flared, and the images dissolved, leaving him breathless but resolute.

Aria was next. She found herself in an endless library, the shelves towering above her and stretching into infinity. The whispers surrounded her, taunting and mocking.

"You think you're clever, but you're nothing." "You failed your parents and failed them, too."

The books began to fall, their pages scattering into ash as the shadows closed in. Aria clenched the journal, her voice steady as she whispered the words of the protective incantation.

"I am more than my fears," she said, her voice growing louder. "I am more than my doubts."

The journal flared with light, and the library dissolved, returning her to the chamber.

Zane stumbled through a dark forest, his breath coming in ragged gasps as the whispers closed around him.

"You left him to die." "You'll leave them, too."

He turned, gripping his hatchet as shadowy figures emerged from the trees, their faces blank and their movements jerky. "I didn't leave him!" he shouted, swinging the hatchet wildly. "I stayed as long as I could!"

The figures surrounded him, their hands reaching out, but Zane planted his feet, his voice defiant. "You're not real! You don't get to tell me who I am!"

The forest dissolved, and Zane was back in the chamber, panting but unbroken.

The Ritual of Courage

The trio reunited in the center of the chamber, their faces pale but determined. The Core pulsed violently, its tendrils lashing out as the whispers reached a deafening crescendo.

"You cannot stop us." "We are eternal."

Aria flipped to the final page of the journal, her voice rising above the chaos. "Theo, the relic! We have to channel its light through the Aegis!"

Theo nodded, holding up the relic as Aria passed him the Aegis. The two objects flared as they touched, their combined light cutting through the darkness like a blade.

"Zane, hold them back!" Theo shouted.

Zane grinned, swinging his hatchet at the tendrils that lunged toward them. "I'm on it!"

Aria began chanting the incantation, her voice clear and confident despite the chaos. The runes carved into the floor began to glow, their light spreading outward as the Core shuddered violently.

The Core's Weakness Revealed

The Core let out a deafening wail as cracks spread across its surface, the light from the Aegis piercing through its defenses.

"You think you are brave," the whispers hissed, their tones fractured and desperate. "But fear is eternal. You cannot destroy it!"

Theo stepped forward, the Aegis blazing in his hand. "You're right," he said. "We can't destroy fear. But we can face it. And we can beat you."

Aria's chanting reached its peak, and the chamber erupted with light. The Core writhed and screamed as its surface shattered, fragments of its energy dissolving into the air.

Cliffhanger

The light from the Aegis dimmed, and the chamber fell silent. The Core was still there, its energy weakened but not gone. The whispers faded into faint murmurs as if retreating.

Aria lowered the journal, her face pale. "We hurt it, but it's not finished."

Zane leaned on his hatchet, his voice tight. "How many lives does this thing have?"

Theo stepped forward, gripping the relic tightly. "One too many. We end this now."

As the trio advanced toward the Core, the chamber walls trembled, and the whispers returned—louder, angrier, and more desperate than ever.

"This is not over."

Chapter 10: The Town's Secret

The trio stumbled out of the Nexus chamber, the oppressive darkness of the Core's lair giving way to the dim, gray light of early dawn filtering through the manor's broken windows. The whispers were quieter now, retreating to the edges of perception like a tide pulling back from the shore.

Zane leaned against the wall, his breathing heavy. "Okay, I think it's safe to say that thing isn't going down without a fight."

Aria flipped through the journal, her brow furrowed. "We weakened it, but the Core is still tethered to something. It's not just the Nexus—it's the entire town."

Theo gripped the relic tightly, its faint glow the only source of comfort. "Then we find what's holding it here and destroy it."

Zane raised an eyebrow. "And how exactly do we do that? Elmwood's not exactly handing out maps to evil anchors."

Aria looked up from the journal, her expression sharp. "No, but the town might have records. The Whisperveil Society was based here for decades. If anyone knew how to fight the Core, it was them."

Theo nodded, his voice steady. "Then we start there."

A Town in Decline

The streets of Elmwood were as lifeless as ever, the faint glow of the morning sun doing little to dispel the eerie stillness that hung over the town. Shuttered windows and crumbling buildings lined the roads, their decay a testament to years of neglect.

As the trio entered the square, a figure stepped out of a nearby alley. It was an older man, his face gaunt and his eyes darting nervously.

"You shouldn't be here," he said, his voice low. "It's not safe."

Theo stepped forward, the relic pulsing faintly in his hand. "We're trying to stop the Core. If you know anything, tell us."

The man shook his head, his expression filled with fear. "The Core can't be stopped. It's been part of this town for as long as I can remember. You'd be better off leaving before it takes you too."

Aria stepped closer, holding up the journal. "The Whisperveil Society fought the Core. They almost stopped it once. Do you know where they kept their records?"

The man hesitated, glancing over his shoulder as if expecting to be watched. Finally, he gestured toward an old stone building on the square's edge.

"The archives," he said. "But you won't like what you find there."

The Hidden Archives

The building was dark and cold, its stone walls lined with shelves of dusty books and crumbling documents. The faint smell of mildew filled the air as Aria began searching the shelves, her fingers brushing over the spines of ancient volumes.

Zane swung his flashlight toward a nearby table, where a stack of yellowed papers lay scattered. "I'm guessing this is where the spooky society kept all their secrets."

Theo picked up a ledger, its leather cover worn and faded. "They weren't just studying the Core—they were feeding it."

Aria turned, her eyes narrowing. "Feeding it?"

Theo held up the ledger, its pages filled with names and dates. "Sacrifices. They were offering up their fears and regrets to keep the Core contained. But it wasn't enough."

Aria scanned a nearby book, her voice trembling. "They thought they could control it. They used symbols and rituals to bind it, but all they did was make it stronger."

Zane frowned, flipping through a journal he had found. "So, they made a deal with a supernatural devil and thought it wouldn't come back to bite them? Classic."

The Final Anchors

Aria's eyes widened as she uncovered a map tucked into one of the books. It was a detailed diagram of Elmwood, marked with the locations of three remaining anchors.

"These are it," she said, pointing to the map. "The last three anchors holding the Core's power in place."

Theo studied the map, his jaw tightening. "The library, the church, and... the cemetery."

Zane groaned, rubbing his temples. "Of course, it's the creepiest place in town. Because why not?"

Aria traced her finger over the map, her expression grim. "If we destroy these, the Core will lose its grip on the town. It'll be vulnerable."

"Then we hit them fast," Theo said, his voice steady. "Before the Core has time to fight back."

The Townsfolk's Warning

As they left the archives, the trio was confronted by a group of townsfolk standing silently in the square. Their expressions were blank, their eyes glowing faintly with the same red light as the Core's tendrils.

"You don't belong here," one of them said, their voice distorted and mechanical.

Theo raised the relic, its light flaring faintly. "We're not leaving."

The townsfolk stepped forward in unison, their movements stiff and unnatural. "The Core will consume you," they said, their voices overlapping in a chilling harmony.

Aria clutched the journal, her voice trembling. "They're echoes. The Core is controlling them."

Zane gripped his hatchet tightly, stepping between Aria and the advancing townsfolk. "Well, they're about to get a serious eviction notice."

Theo held up the relic, its light creating a barrier between the trio and the echoes. "We're not here to hurt you. But we're not letting the Core win."

The whispers surged, and the townsfolk froze, their glowing eyes flickering. Then, as if retreating, they stepped back into the shadows, disappearing as suddenly as they had appeared.

Cliffhanger

The trio stood in silence, the tension thick in the air.

"They'll be back," Aria said softly, her grip on the journal tightening.

Theo nodded, his gaze fixed on the map in his hand. "Then we need to move. The Core's not going to wait for us to finish this."

Zane smirked faintly, though his eyes were serious. "Guess it's time for the graveyard shift."

The whispers rose as they approached the first anchor, faint and mocking.

"You cannot sever us." "You will fall."

Theo gripped the relic tightly, his voice firm. "Not this time."

The trio disappeared into the shadows of the town, their footsteps fading as the whispers followed them into the growing dawn.

Chapter 11: A Dark Revelation

The trio moved cautiously through the streets of Elmwood, the map clutched tightly in Theo's hand. The faint light of dawn did little to dispel the shadows that seemed to cling to the edges of every building, nor did it silence the whispers that followed them like a low, ever-present hum.

"The first anchor is the library," Aria said, her voice steady but quiet. She pointed toward the weathered stone building at the center of the square. "If we can destroy it, the Core's grip on the town will weaken."

Theo nodded, his jaw tightening. "Let's move quickly. The Core's going to fight back harder than ever."

"Good," Zane said, swinging his hatchet onto his shoulder. "I owe it for the last couple of nightmares."

The Library's Secrets

Inside the library, the air was colder than before, carrying the faint metallic tang of blood. The whispers grew louder as they stepped inside, the relic's light flickering faintly in Theo's hand.

Aria flipped through the journal, her brow furrowing. "The anchor should be beneath the foundation. We need to find the access point."

"Access point?" Zane repeated, his flashlight sweeping across the dusty floor. "How about a trapdoor that says 'Insert Heroes Here'?"

Theo scanned the room, his gaze falling on a faint outline in the floorboards near the librarian's counter. He knelt, brushing away years of dust to reveal a small hatch with runes carved into its surface.

"This is it," Theo said, gripping the relic tightly.

Aria knelt beside him, tracing the runes with her fingers. "These symbols are different. They're meant to ward off intruders, not the Core."

Zane leaned over them, his voice tense. "Yeah, well, they're not exactly working, are they?"

The runes flared suddenly, a blinding light erupting from the hatch. The whispers became a deafening roar, and the room trembled violently.

The Echoes Attack

Dark figures emerged from the shadows, their hollow eyes glowing faintly.

"They're echoes!" Aria shouted, scrambling to her feet.

Zane swung his hatchet at the nearest figure, his voice rising above the chaos. "Guess it's my turn to check out some books!"

The echo dissolved into mist as his blade struck, but two more took its place, their movements jerky and unnatural.

Theo raised the relic, its light flaring brightly. The echoes recoiled, their forms flickering like faulty projections, but they quickly regrouped.

"They're stalling us," Aria said, her voice steady as she flipped to a page in the journal. "If I can disable the runes, we can get to the anchor!"

"Do it fast!" Theo shouted, stepping between her and the advancing echoes.

Disabling the Anchor's Defenses

Aria knelt by the hatch, her fingers moving quickly as she traced over the runes with a piece of chalk from her bag. The whispers shifted, their tones turning mocking and cruel.

"You'll fail." "You're not strong enough." "Give up while you can."

Aria's hands trembled, but she kept working, her voice steady. "I'm not listening to you."

Theo swung the relic toward the echoes, its light slicing through their forms. "Zane, on your left!"

Zane turned, his hatchet connecting with another echo as it lunged for him. "These things are like cockroaches!"

The final rune flared as Aria finished the chalk markings, and the hatch clicked open.

"Got it!" she shouted, standing quickly.

The Anchor Beneath the Library

The hatch revealed a narrow staircase leading into darkness. The air grew colder as they descended, and the whispers intensified with every step.

At the bottom, the anchor stood in the center of the room: a jagged crystal pulsing faintly with light, its surface etched with runes. Dark roots twisted around its base, glowing faintly with the same malevolent energy as the Core.

"This is it," Theo said, steadily. "One of the final anchors."

Aria opened the journal, her eyes scanning the page. "The ritual to destroy it requires all three of us. We must focus on the relic and use Aegis to channel its energy."

Theo nodded, holding up the relic. "Let's do it."

As Aria began the incantation, the roots surrounding the anchor writhed violently, lashing out like tendrils desperate to defend their source, striking the air with wild abandon. Shadows deepened around them, pulsating with the Core's ominous energy. Theo gripped the glowing relic tightly, as he said, **"Aria, keep going! It's working!"**

The Anchor's Last Stand

As Aria continued the incantation, the roots surrounding the anchor writhed violently, lashing out like tendrils.

Theo stepped forward, raising the relic to shield her. "Keep going!"

Zane swung his hatchet, severing one of the roots as it lunged for them. "This thing really doesn't **want to let go!"**

The anchor pulsed brighter, and a surge of energy knocked the trio back. The room trembled.

"You cannot win." "This is our domain." "You will fail."

Aria pushed herself up, her voice rising above the chaos as she continued the chant. The runes on the anchor began to crack, light spilling from the fractures.

Theo and Zane moved to shield her, their combined efforts pushing back the roots as the anchor shuddered violently.

A Dark Revelation

As the final word of the incantation left Aria's lips, the anchor shattered, releasing a shockwave of light and shadow that sent them sprawling.

The whispers fell silent, but Theo's chest tightened as he pushed himself to his feet. A faint glow lingered in the shattered remains of the anchor, and an image began to form.

It was Amelia.

Her ghostly form flickered faintly, her eyes filled with sadness. "It's not just the Core," she said, trembling. "The anchors... they were part of the veil's balance. Without them, the Core will lash out even harder."

Aria's voice wavered. "But we have to destroy the anchors to stop it."

Amelia nodded slowly, her expression grim. "You must sever its ties to the town, but the Core won't go quietly. It's already preparing for you."

Zane's face hardened. "Good. Let it prepare. We'll be ready."

Cliffhanger

The glow from the shattered anchor faded, and Amelia's ghost dissolved into light.

Theo turned to his friends, forcing calm into his voice. "Two more anchors. We take them out, and this ends."

Aria clutched the journal tightly, her face pale but determined. "We have to be careful. The Core is going to throw everything it has at us now."

Zane smirked faintly, though his grip on his hatchet tightened. "Bring it on."

The trio ascended the stairs, the whispers stirring faintly as they stepped back into the quiet streets of Elmwood. Above them, the sky darkened, and a low rumble of thunder echoed in the distance.

The Core was waiting.

Chapter 12: Bonds of Friendship

The storm over Elmwood broke as the trio left the library, dark clouds swirling ominously overhead. Thunder rumbled in the distance, and the air carried a charge that prickled against their skin. The whispers had grown fainter but more insidious, their tones weaving doubts and fears into the silence.

"We're running out of time," Aria said, clutching the journal tightly. "The Core knows we're coming. It's preparing for us."

Zane swung his hatchet in a wide arc, his tension apparent. "Let it prepare. We've already taken down two anchors. What's one more?"

"It's not just one more," Theo said, his voice held firm but strained. He gripped the relic tightly, its light flickering in his hand. "This next anchor is the church. It's probably the most protected of all."

Aria looked up at the darkened sky, her expression somber. "We've weakened the Core, but it's still feeding on fear. It's going to try to divide us. We have to stay together."

Zane smirked faintly, though his eyes betrayed his unease. "No one's going anywhere. We've come too far to let some creepy shadow monster get between us."

The Church of Shadows

The old stone church loomed ahead, its spire piercing the stormy sky like a jagged spear. The stained-glass windows were cracked and dark, their images twisted into grotesque versions of saints and angels.

The trio paused at the entrance, the heavy wooden doors bound with glowing roots that pulsed faintly with light.

"This is it," Theo said, stepping forward. The relic flared in his hand, and the roots recoiled slightly, hissing as they shrank back.

Aria flipped to a page in the journal, her brow furrowing. "The church was built on one of the strongest ley lines in town. The Whisperveil Society used it as a focal point to channel their rituals."

"Great," Zane said, gripping his hatchet tightly. "So, what's the over-under on this place being a total nightmare?"

Theo pushed open the doors, the relic's light casting long shadows across the pews. "Only one way to find out."

The Heart of the Anchor

The church's interior was cold and silent, the air thick with the scent of decay. Rows of pews lined the nave, their wood splintered and rotting. At the far end, the altar stood beneath a massive stained-glass window, its surface crawling with dark roots.

Above the altar, a glowing crystal pulsed faintly, its light casting eerie patterns across the walls.

"There it is," Aria whispered, pointing to the crystal. "The third anchor."

The whispers grew louder as the trio approached the altar, their tones sharp and mocking.

"You cannot sever us." "We are eternal." "Turn back or be consumed."

Theo raised the relic, its light flaring as the whispers surged. "We're not turning back."

The Core's Defense

As Aria began to read the incantation from the journal, the church erupted in chaos. The stained-glass window shattered, and shadowy figures poured through the gaping hole, their hollow eyes glowing faintly.

"They're not wasting time, are they?" Zane said, stepping in front of Aria. He swung his hatchet at the first figure, its form dissolving into mist only to reform seconds later.

"They're echoes!" Aria shouted, her voice trembling as she continued the chant. "Just keep them off me!"

Theo stepped beside Zane, the relic's light pushing back the advancing echoes. "We have to hold them here. Aria needs time."

The echoes swarmed, their movements erratic and unnatural. Theo and Zane fought side by side, their strikes precise but desperate as the shadows closed in.

The Power of Friendship

Aria's voice rose above the chaos, her chant growing more assertive as she drew power from the runes on the journal's pages.

The crystal began to crack, its light dimming as the energy around it wavered. The whispers turned to screams, their tones angry and desperate.

"You cannot destroy us." "We are your fear." "We are your truth."

Theo staggered as one of the echoes lashed out, its shadowy claws raking across his arm. The relic flared in his hand, forcing the figure back, but the pain was sharp and real.

"You okay?" Zane asked, swinging his hatchet at another echo.

"I'm fine," Theo said through gritted teeth. "Just keep them back."

Zane grinned, though his movements were more frantic now. "Don't worry, Captain Courage. I've got your back."

The Breaking Point

As the anchor's light dimmed further, the room trembled violently. The shadows grew more aggressive, their forms twisting into monstrous shapes.

Aria faltered, her voice shaking as the whispers surged. "They're trying to stop me!"

Theo turned to her, his voice firm. "You can do this, Aria. Don't let them in."

Zane stepped in front of her, his hatchet raised. "She's not going anywhere. You hear that, you creepy jerks? Back off!"

The relic's light flared brighter, and Theo stepped toward the altar, raising it high. "We're stronger than you," he said, his voice held firm. "We're stronger together."

The crystal let out a deafening wail as it shattered, releasing a wave of light that swept through the church. The echoes dissolved into mist, and the whispers fell silent.

Aftermath

Aria lowered the journal, her breathing heavy. "We did it," she said softly, her voice trembling with relief.

Theo nodded, though his grip on the relic remained tight. "That's three anchors down. The Core is running out of places to hide."

Zane leaned against a pew, his face pale but determined. "Yeah, but it won't go down without a fight. That thing's probably furious."

Aria glanced at the shattered remains of the anchor, her expression somber. "We're getting close. We have to keep pushing."

Cliffhanger

As the trio stepped out of the church, the storm overhead intensified. Lightning flashed across the sky, illuminating the twisted shadows that seemed to writhe along the edges of the square.

The whispers returned, louder and angrier than ever.

"You will not escape." "This is where it ends."

Theo tightened his grip on the relic. "Then we finish this."

The trio moved toward the cemetery, their resolve unshaken even as the shadows followed them, the whispers echoing in their wake.

Chapter 13: The Core Confronted

The cemetery loomed ahead, its iron gates twisted and rusted with age. Thick fog curled around the headstones, and the air was heavy with the scent of damp earth. Beyond the crumbling mausoleums and leaning crosses, the Core's pulsing light emanated faintly from the depths of the ground, like a heartbeat vibrating through the earth.

"This is it," Theo said, his voice steady despite the moment's weight. "The final anchor."

Aria held the journal tightly, her knuckles white. "Once we destroy it, the Core will be vulnerable. But the veil will throw everything at us to stop that from happening."

Zane swung his hatchet in a slow arc, his grin faint but resolute. "Good. I was starting to miss the swarm of creepy shadows."

The relic in Theo's hand flared faintly, and he stepped forward, pushing open the cemetery gate. "Let's finish this."

The Core's Last Anchor

The trio moved cautiously through the cemetery, their footsteps crunching against the gravel path. The whispers surrounded them, louder now than ever, their tones furious and mocking.

"You think you can destroy us?" "We are your fear. We are your truth." "You cannot escape."

The final anchor was embedded at the base of a massive tree at the center of the cemetery. Its twisted roots crawled across the ground, pulsing with the same red light as the Core. The crystal glowed faintly, its surface etched with runes that shimmered ominously.

Aria flipped through the journal, her eyes scanning the pages. "This ritual is different," she said, her voice tight. "The last anchor is directly tied to the Core. Destroying it will sever the veil's power over the town but also trigger the Core's full retaliation."

Zane raised an eyebrow. "Translation?"

Aria looked up, her expression grim. "Once we destroy this anchor, there's no turning back."

The Core Strikes First

Before they could begin the ritual, the ground beneath them trembled violently, and the whispers became a deafening roar. Shadows erupted from the ground like jagged spears, their tendrils lashing out at the trio.

"Move!" Theo shouted, raising the relic. Its light flared, forcing the shadows to retreat, but they quickly reformed, their movements faster and more aggressive.

Aria scrambled back, clutching the journal. "It's defending the anchor! I need time to start the incantation!"

Zane swung his hatchet at the nearest shadow, cutting through its form. "Time we don't have!"

Theo stepped between Aria and the advancing shadows, the relic blazing in his hand. "We'll hold them off. Just focus on the ritual!"

A Desperate Battle

The shadows swarmed, their movements erratic and relentless. Theo and Zane fought side by side, their strikes coordinated but desperate as the veil's defenses grew more frenzied.

Zane swung his hatchet at a tendril, his voice rising above the chaos. "These things just keep coming!"

Theo gritted his teeth, the relic flaring brightly as he pushed back another wave. "They're buying time for the Core. We can't let them stop us now."

Aria knelt by the anchor, her voice steady as she began the incantation. The runes on the crystal started to glow brighter, their light flickering as the ritual progressed.

The whispers shifted, their tones turning pleading.

"Stop!" "You don't understand!" "This will destroy you!"

Aria's voice rose above them, unwavering. "We're not afraid of you."

The Anchor Breaks

As the final word of the incantation left Aria's lips, the anchor let out a deafening wail. The crystal cracked, light spilling from its surface as the roots surrounding it withered and disintegrated.

The shadows let out a collective scream, their forms dissolving into mist as the ground beneath the trio shuddered violently.

"It's breaking!" Theo shouted, gripping the relic tightly as the anchor shattered completely. A shockwave of light and shadow erupted from the crystal, throwing them to the ground.

The whispers fell silent, and the cemetery was still for a moment.

The Core Confronted

The stillness was short-lived. The light in the distance pulsed violently, and the whispers returned, louder and more chaotic than ever.

"You have made a grave mistake." "This is where it ends."

Theo pushed himself to his feet, his chest tightening as the relic flared brightly. "The Core's coming. It knows we're coming for it."

Aria stood, brushing dirt from her knees. "The final confrontation. This is what Amelia was preparing us for."

Zane gripped his hatchet, his smirk faint but determined. "Let's make it regret ever messing with this town."

The trio turned toward the source of the light, the Core's pulsating glow illuminating the darkened sky. The whispers surrounded them, overlapping in a deafening chorus as the ground beneath them crumbled.

"The veil will consume you." "This is your end."

Theo gripped the relic tightly, the fear curling in his chest. "Not this time."

Cliffhanger

As they advanced toward the Core, the storm overhead reached a fever pitch. Lightning illuminated the twisted landscape, and the Core's form became clearer—a massive, writhing sphere of light and shadow, its surface alive with distorted faces and jagged tendrils.

The whispers became a single, booming voice, its tone filled with rage.

"You cannot destroy fear. You cannot destroy me!"

Theo raised the relic, its light blazing brightly as they stepped into the heart of the storm.

"We're not here to destroy you," he said, unwaveringly. "We're here to end you."

The Core shuddered violently, and the trio disappeared into the blinding light as the storm erupted around them.

Chapter 14: Shattered Illusions

The Core's chamber was a nightmare come to life. The walls twisted and writhed, their surfaces covered in glowing runes that pulsed like living veins. The ground beneath the trio's feet cracked and shifted like a fragile shell, barely containing the chaos in the room.

In the center of the chamber, the Core floated—a massive, pulsating sphere of light and shadow. Its surface shimmered with distorted faces, their expressions twisting in anguish as tendrils of dark energy lashed out wildly.

The whispers filled the air, louder than ever, their overlapping voices cutting into Theo, Aria, and Zane like icy knives.

"You cannot defeat us." "You are nothing without your fear." "This is the end."

Theo gripped the relic tightly, its light flaring as he stepped forward. "We've come too far to stop now."

Aria clutched the journal, her voice steady. "This is its last defense. It's trying to break us."

Zane swung his hatchet in a wide arc, his tension evident in his movements. "Let it try. We're not going anywhere."

The Core's Assault

The Core shuddered violently, and the chamber erupted in chaos. Tendrils of shadow lashed out from its surface, slamming into the walls and ground with enough force to send cracks splintering across the floor.

Theo raised the relic, its light cutting through the darkness as one of the tendrils lunged toward them. "Stay close!" he shouted, his voice rising above the whispers.

Aria flipped to a page in the journal, scanning the runes. "It's warping the space around us. We must disrupt its hold on the chamber before striking at the Core itself!"

"Any ideas on how we do that?" Zane asked, dodging a tendril that narrowly missed his shoulder.

"The runes!" Aria shouted, pointing to the glowing symbols on the walls. "They're feeding it power. If we can break them, we can weaken it."

Theo nodded, his gaze sharp. "Zane, cover her. I'll handle the relic."

Zane smirked faintly, his hatchet gleaming in the relic's light. "You got it, boss."

Breaking the Runes

As Aria began tracing the runes with chalk, the chamber seemed to sense her actions. The tendrils became more frantic, their strikes faster and more precise.

"You cannot sever us." "This is your end."

Zane swung his hatchet at a tendril, severing it with a grunt of effort. "You're going to have to work faster, Aria!"

"I'm doing my best!" she shot back, her hand moving quickly as she completed the first rune. The moment the chalk connected the final line, the symbol on the wall flared brightly before shattering like glass.

The Core let out a deafening roar, and the tendrils recoiled slightly.

"It's working!" Theo shouted, raising the relic to hold back another wave of shadows. "Keep going!"

The Core's Illusions

The chamber twisted suddenly, and Theo felt the ground disappear beneath his feet. He blinked, disoriented, as the familiar surroundings of the chamber dissolved into a fragmented vision.

He was back in the manor's foyer before the broken mirror. Amelia's reflection stared at him, her eyes wide with fear.

"You couldn't save me," her voice echoed, trembling and broken. "And you can't save them."

"No," Theo said, gripping the relic tightly. "This isn't real."

The mirror shattered, and the fragments swirled around him, each reflecting his face, twisted in anguish.

Aria found herself alone in the manor's library, the shelves towering above her. Books tumbled to the ground, their pages dissolving into ash. A figure appeared in the distance, its features obscured, but its voice was unmistakable.

"You hide behind knowledge, but it won't protect you," it said, its tone cold and mocking.

Aria clenched her fists, her voice steady. "I'm not hiding. I'm fighting."

The library dissolved, and she forced herself back into the chamber, her determination more potent than ever.

Zane staggered as the chamber dissolved into a hospital room. He instantly recognized the stark white walls, the beeping machines, and the still figure lying in the bed.

"You left me," the figure rasped, sitting up slowly.

"No," Zane said, his voice shaking. "I didn't leave you. I stayed as long as I could."

The figure's face contorted, its voice rising into a menacing echo. "You'll abandon them, too—just like you abandoned me."

Zane swung his hatchet at the apparition, his voice rising. "I'm not leaving anyone!"

The hospital room shattered, and Zane returned to the chamber, panting but resolute.

United Again

The trio reappeared in the chamber, their faces pale but determined. The Core shuddered violently, its surface cracking as the final rune shattered.

Aria clutched the journal, her voice trembling but strong. "The chamber's weakened. We can finish this."

Theo raised the relic, its light flaring brightly. "Together."

Zane smirked, stepping forward. "Let's show this thing what it gets for messing with us."

Cliffhanger

The Core's surface cracked further, and a surge of energy erupted from it, engulfing the chamber in blinding light. The whispers turned into a single, booming voice.

"You think you are strong?" it roared, its tone filled with fury. "You cannot destroy fear. You cannot destroy me!"

Theo gripped the relic tightly, stepping forward as the light surrounded them. "We don't have to destroy you," he said. "We just have to break free."

The chamber trembled, and the trio disappeared into the Core's light as the whispers erupted around them.

Uneasy glances passed between them as the first whispers returned—faint but unmistakable—carried on the wind.

Chapter 15: Becoming the Light

The light was blinding. Theo, Aria, and Zane felt weightless momentarily, as if they had been pulled into an infinite void. The whispers were no longer distant—they surrounded them completely, their tones sharp and accusatory, overlapping into a chaotic symphony.

"You are nothing." "You cannot win." "This is the end."

Theo gripped the relic tightly, its faint glow barely visible against the overwhelming brightness. "Stay together!" he shouted, his voice cutting through the din. "We don't let go!"

Aria reached for Zane's hand, her grip firm. "We've come too far to lose each other now."

Zane nodded, gripping Theo's arm to form a chain. "Whatever this thing has planned, it's not splitting us up."

The trio braced themselves as the light began to shift, revealing the heart of the Core.

The Heart of the Core

The trio stood in a cavernous space that defied logic. The walls shimmered like liquid, pulsating with light and shadow that twisted together in an endless dance. At the center of the room, the Core loomed larger than ever, its surface cracked but alive with writhing tendrils and distorted faces.

The whispers converged into a single, booming voice that echoed through the chamber.

"You cannot destroy fear. It is eternal. It is you."

Aria stepped forward, clutching the journal tightly. "You're wrong," she said, her voice steady. "Fear isn't eternal. It's a shadow. And shadows can't survive the light."

The Core shuddered violently, its tendrils lashing out. Theo raised the relic, its light flaring to block the attack.

"It's afraid of us," Theo said, his voice firm. "That's why it's lashing out. It knows we're strong enough to break it."

Zane grinned, raising his hatchet. "Then let's show it what happens when you mess with the wrong people."

The Keeper's Aegis

The relic glowed brighter as Theo stepped forward, holding it high. The Keeper's Aegis, embedded within the relic, began to glow, its light cutting through the shadows and illuminating the room.

Aria flipped to the final page of the journal, her hands trembling but steady. "The ritual to sever the Core's power—it's going to take everything we've got."

Theo nodded, his gaze unwavering. "We're ready."

The Core let out a deafening roar, its surface cracking further as its tendrils lashed out. "You cannot sever me!" it screamed. "I am your truth! I am your fear!"

Zane swung his hatchet at an approaching tendril, slicing through it. "Yeah, yeah. We've heard it all before!"

The Final Ritual

Aria began to chant, her voice rising above the chaos. The runes on the relic flared, and the Core recoiled as the light intensified.

Theo held the relic steady, its light pouring into the room and forcing the shadows to retreat. "Zane, keep them off her!"

"On it!" Zane shouted, his movements swift as he cut through the tendrils that lunged toward them.

The Core writhed, its form flickering as cracks spread across its surface. The faces within it screamed silently, their anguish echoing through the chamber.

"You are weak," the Core hissed, its voice trembling. "You cannot destroy what you are."

Aria's chant grew louder, her voice filled with conviction. "We're not destroying fear. We're breaking free from it."

United as One

The light from the relic and the Aegis began to merge, forming a sphere of pure energy that radiated warmth and hope. Theo's grip on the relic tightened, and he turned to his friends.

"This isn't just my fight," he said, his voice steady. "It's ours. We've faced our fears and are stronger because of it."

Aria placed her hand on the relic, her expression resolute. "We're stronger together."

Zane stepped forward, gripping the relic as well. "Let's end this."

The light flared, and the whispers turned into a deafening wail as the Core began to shatter.

The Core's Collapse

The Core's surface cracked and splintered, its tendrils disintegrating into ash. The faces within it dissolved, their anguished expressions replaced by fleeting smiles of relief.

"You cannot..." the Core's voice faltered, its tone desperate. "You will fall... without me."

Theo stepped forward, the relic blazing in his hands. "We're not falling. We're rising."

With a final surge of energy, the trio directed the light into the Core, its form collapsing. The chamber trembled violently, and the whispers ceased as the Core exploded into a wave of light.

Aftermath

The trio found themselves standing in the chamber's ruins. The walls no longer pulsed with shadow, and the air was still. The relic in Theo's hand was dim but warm, its light a faint but steady glow.

Aria looked around, her voice soft. "It's gone. The Core... the veil... it's all gone."

Zane leaned on his hatchet, his breathing heavy. "We actually did it. We beat that thing."

Theo nodded, a faint smile crossing his face. "We didn't just beat it. We freed everyone it was holding."

Cliffhanger

As they stepped out of the ruins, the storm overhead began to clear, revealing a sky painted with soft hues of dawn. The whispers were gone, replaced by a profound silence.

But as Theo turned the relic in his hands, a faint symbol appeared on its surface—a mark that had never been there before.

"What is that?" Aria asked, her voice filled with curiosity and unease.

Theo stared at the mark, his expression unreadable. "I don't know. But I think... it's not over."

Zane frowned, his grip tightening on his hatchet. "Well, whatever's next, we'll face it. Together."

The trio stood beneath the rising sun, the relic's light a beacon against the uncertainty ahead.

Chapter 16: The Light Beyond

The morning sun crept over the ruins of Elmwood Manor, its golden light cutting through the lingering fog and bathing the crumbling walls in a warm glow. The air felt lighter, the oppressive weight of the whispers finally gone.

Theo, Aria, and Zane stood at the edge of the ruined chamber, the relic glowing faintly in Theo's hand. Around them, the remnants of the Core's influence crumbled into dust, its dark tendrils dissolving into nothingness.

"We did it," Aria said softly, her voice filled with awe. "It's really over."

Zane wiped the sweat from his brow, leaning on his hatchet with a faint grin. "You sound surprised. What, didn't think we'd make it this far?"

Aria gave him a small smile. "I wasn't doubting us. But after everything we've faced, it's hard to believe we won."

Theo glanced at the relic, its light steady but dim. "It's more than a win," he said. "We freed Amelia. We freed the town. And we broke the Core's hold for good."

A Town Awakened

As they returned to Elmwood, the town was almost unrecognizable. The heavy stillness that had shrouded the streets was gone, replaced by a sense of quiet renewal. Windows that had been boarded up were now open, and the faint sounds of life returned as townsfolk stepped hesitantly outside.

An older woman approached the trio, her face lined with years of worry. "It's... gone," she said, her voice trembling. "The whispers... they've stopped."

"They won't come back," Theo assured her, his voice steady. "The Core is destroyed. The town is free."

The woman's eyes filled with tears as she placed a hand over her heart. "Thank you. You've saved us all."

Aria smiled, small and proud, at Theo. "You really did it," she said. "We all did."

Amelia's Farewell

A faint shimmer appeared before them as they approached the edge of the forest. Amelia's ghostly form emerged from the trees, her braided hair glowing softly in the sunlight.

"Amelia," Theo said, stepping forward.

She smiled, her eyes filled with gratitude. "You kept your promise," she said. "You freed me. And you freed them."

Aria's voice was gentle. "What happens now?"

Amelia glanced toward the horizon, where the forest seemed to dissolve into light. "I can finally rest," she said. "But the veil... it's bigger than this town. There are other places like Elmwood. Other Cores, other whispers."

Theo tightened his grip on the relic, the faint symbol etched into its surface catching the light. "And we'll find them. We'll stop them, too."

Amelia nodded, her form beginning to fade. "Thank you," she said, her voice soft and transparent. "For giving me hope."

As she disappeared, a warm breeze swept through the forest, carrying the scent of blooming flowers.

A New Beginning

The trio stood silently for a moment, the weight of their journey settling over them.

Zane broke the quiet with a smirk. "So... does this mean we're officially professional ghost hunters now? Or do we get a break first?"

Aria rolled her eyes, but her smile was genuine. "I think we've earned a break. At least until the next mysterious relic shows up."

Theo chuckled, slipping the relic into his pocket. "Let's just get back to town. There's probably a lot of cleanup to do."

As they walked back toward Elmwood, the sunlight grew brighter, casting away the last traces of the veil.

Epilogue: A Whisper in the Wind

Months later, Theo stood on the cliff overlooking the ruins of the manor, the relic resting in his palm. The symbol etched into its surface glowed faintly, a reminder of the journey they had taken—and the challenges that lay ahead.

A faint breeze stirred the air, carrying with it a familiar voice.

"Thank you, Theo... for setting us free."

He smiled, closing his fingers around the relic. Behind him, Aria and Zane waited, their faces alight with determination.

"Ready?" Aria asked, her voice steady.

"Always," Theo said, turning to join them.

The trio walked toward the horizon, their path illuminated by the morning sun, ready to face whatever awaited them beyond the veil.

Author's Note

Dear Reader,

Writing Whisperveil: The Light Beyond has been an incredible journey. As my debut novel, this story represents a dream turned into reality—a first step into the world of storytelling that I've always hoped to share with readers like you.

Like all firsts, it came with challenges, doubts, and whispers of uncertainty. But I believe courage is born when one steps into the unknown, and this book is proof of that.

I wanted to create a tale that challenges the mind, uplifts the spirit, and reminds us all that no matter how loud fear may seem, the light within us—and the people we lean on—is stronger.

To anyone who has ever faced doubt or fear, know that you're not alone. And to those who believe in me—thank you for walking alongside me on this journey.

This is only the beginning. Keep seeking the light, and thank you for allowing me to share my first story with you.

With gratitude, Jah Kingdom